Five-Minute Chillers

By William A. Walker, Jr.

Illustrated by
Brian Dow

Sterling Publishing Co., Inc.
New York

To my parents, Jane and Bill. From the bottom of my heart, I thank you for my talents and your unceasing faith in them.

—W.A.W., Jr.

To my wife, Karen, who is the light along the path to fulfilling our dreams.

—B.W.D.

Library of Congress Cataloging-in-Publication Data Available

10 9 8 7 6 5 4 3 2 1

Published by Sterling Publishing Company, Inc.
387 Park Avenue South, New York, N.Y. 10016
© 1995 by RGA Publishing, Inc.
Distributed in Canada by Sterling Publishing
c/o Canadian Manda Group, One Atlantic Avenue, Suite 105
Toronto, Ontario, Canada M6K 3E7
Distributed in Great Britain and Europe by Cassell PLC
Wellington House, 125 Strand, London WC2R 0BB, England
Distributed in Australia by Capricorn Link (Australia) Pty Ltd.
P.O. Box 6651, Baulkham Hills, Business Centre, NSW 2153, Australia
Manufactured in the United States of America

Sterling ISBN 0-8069-0954-4 Trade
      0-8069-0955-2 Paper

Table of Contents

Thirteen Minutes to Kill

etty's eyes blazed. "There is *so* a treasure in the swamp. Amy Monniker said it was gold meant for the Confederate Army. They say it's still out there, guarded by an army of gray ghosts."

"Oh, Betty," her brother Billy said, rolling his eyes. "I can't believe you bought into Motormouth Monniker's baloney. She's a worse tall-tale-teller than you."

"That's tellin' her, Billy Boy," Gary said, holding his chubby belly as he giggled. "You probably believe there's gold in the swamp yourself."

"Stuff it, Gary," Billy said, good-naturedly. Friends since they could walk, Billy and Gary enjoyed constantly ribbing each other.

Gary's eyebrows shot up. "Well, if there is a treasure in the swamp, tonight is the night to go for it. . . . "In case you guys forgot, it's Friday the thirteenth."

Billy stared at Gary. "So?"

"Aw, come on, Billy Boy. Everyone knows that's the one day the gray ghosts have the night off. According to the legend, anyone who can grab the loot before midnight has got it made . . . *if* they get out in time." Gary's expression turned wicked. "I'll bring shovels. Are you guys coming with me?"

"I am!" Betty exclaimed, clapping her hands.

"Me, too," Billy said, a little reluctantly.

After arguing about where they would meet and at what time, the group decided to rendezvous at the south end of the swamp at 10:30 that night. "That should give us enough time to find the treasure and blow outta there before midnight," Gary reasoned. "But we'd all better wear our running shoes."

A full moon hung overhead when Billy and Betty crept out of their house later that night. Stifling giggles, they ran the quarter mile to the south end of Sanford Swamp, where Gary was already waiting.

"Thought you guys were gonna chicken out on me." Gary gestured toward the swamp. "Pretty cool, huh?"

Though less than a square mile wide, the swamp appeared to stretch to the horizon. Clumps of sickly grass dotted the areas between bogs, and what few trees existed had died long ago, leaving only rotting hulks that jutted out of the stagnant water like lonely sentries guarding nothing. A faint, glowing mist hugged the ground, and the smell of rotten eggs hung in the air.

Betty shook her head. "I'm not going in there."

Gary looked annoyed. "I knew she'd chicken out."

Billy stared daggers at Gary, causing the other boy to cast his eyes downward. "Come on, Betty," Billy pleaded. "You can't quit on me now!"

Shrugging, Betty grabbed the flashlight out of his hand and began clambering over the barbed wire.

As they trekked through the swamp, Billy, the only one who'd worn a watch, kept checking the time to make sure they got out by midnight. On and on they walked, their feet sloshing through the muck, but there was no sign of anything that resembled a treasure. Billy

6

checked his watch again. It was already 11:45 and they'd found nothing—a big, fat zero.

"Are you satisfied?" Billy asked his sister as he leaned against the rotted hulk of an old ash tree. "Your friend Amy is an idiot!"

Betty scowled. "Look who's talking. I don't see *her* out here. And who was it that was supposed to bring the shovels?"

Their eyes shifted to Gary, who tried to look innocent. "Hey, my dad has the keys to the toolshed. How'd I know he'd be out of town tonight?"

"Never mind," Billy said. "Let's just get out of this place."

But as they turned, a light began to glow through the trees. In a moment, it grew so bright that the three of them had to squint. And then they saw it.

There, in a clearing, was an ancient iron strongbox, its lid lying open. And something was pulsing inside, glowing with a golden radiance.

Gary whooped with joy. "Thar she blows!" And with that, he began to run through the swamp toward the unearthly light.

Betty grabbed Billy's arm. "What time is it?"

"Thirteen minutes till midnight," he said excitedly. "We still have time to kill!"

"No we don't," she warned, gripping his arm tighter.

With a look that asked if she were crazy, Billy tore loose from his sister's grasp and dashed after Gary, his own laughter mingling with his friend's.

Afraid for her brother, Betty ran after them, and as she drew closer to the box, she could see that it was filled with hundreds of gold coins. The treasure

seemed to pulsate even more the nearer she got to the box, drawing her toward it, making her want it.

"We're filthy stinkin' rich!" Gary cried, letting the shiny coins slither through his fingers.

Billy joined him. "Come on, Betty, help us!" Billy yelled, looking over his shoulder at his sister. "You're missing out on all the—" But Betty's haunted look caused Billy to stop what he was doing. "What is it, Betty?" he asked. "What's wrong?"

"We have to go, Billy—*now*!" Betty cried.

"But we've still got ten minutes," Billy insisted, showing her the lighted dial on his digital wristwatch.

"You don't understand!" Betty screamed. "I—I forgot that I played a joke on you, and I—I set your watch and alarm clock back fifteen minutes. That means it's already five minutes *after* midnight!"

Billy's eyes bulged as the sound of a distant bugle call pierced the air. All around them the mist began to move, taking on the shapes of men. In a moment the kids were surrounded by an army of Confederate soldiers, their ragged uniforms decayed and teeming with maggots.

An officer, his face a mass of rotting flesh, stepped forward, proudly wearing his plumed hat.

"Gentlemen," he said to his troops, his golden eyes glowing with mad-eyed triumph, "our replacements have finally arrived!"

Uncle Alfred's Time Machine

Uncle Alfred grabbed his remote control. "Stand back! This is history in the making!"

Ten-year-old Reggie pulled his helmet lower onto his face. He knew from experience that anything his eccentric uncle invented was more likely to blow up, shake apart, or fizzle than it was to work.

"What do you call this thing, Uncle Albert?" Reggie asked, staring at the machine that sat in Alfred's backyard, bleeping, clanking, and whirling. It looked like a bunch of household items: old-fashioned toasters, Christmas-tree lights, vacuum cleaner parts, and what appeared to be a sewing machine motor, all welded together into a phantasmic sculpture.

The older man looked surprised for a second, then smiled. "Why, it's a genuine, newfangled *Gonkulator*!"

Reggie looked puzzled. "What does it do?"

Alfred scratched his gray head. "Why, I don't know. But whatever it does, we'll be the first to see." He gripped the remote control in his gnarled hands. "Ready, Captain Video?" he called, turning to Reggie.

Reggie nodded, brought the camcorder up to his face, and pushed the RECORD button. "Rolling!" he yelled.

"T minus five," Uncle Alfred counted, "four . . . three . . . two . . . ONE!" He pressed the button on the remote control and a loud beep pierced the air.

Suddenly, the Gonkulator began to shimmy, emitting a sharp, burbling sound, like the cry of some mechanized baby. Then, in a flash of light, the entire contraption exploded, launching debris in every direction and sending Reggie and his uncle dodging for cover.

After a moment, Uncle Alfred stood up and sighed. "Back to the drawing board."

Reggie followed his dejected uncle back into the dilapidated garage he used as his lab, careful to duck, lest he hit his head on all the junk hanging from the beams. The old man sat at his bench, his face in his hands, suddenly looking a thousand years old.

Feeling sorry for him, Reggie laid his hand on his uncle's bony shoulder. "It's okay, Uncle Alfred," he said encouragingly. "You'll do better next time."

Alfred's watery hazel eyes peered into Reggie's soul. "Nothing I've ever done has amounted to a hill of beans," he said, pausing. "Except this."

He walked over to a dusty tarp and whisked it aside, revealing a machine unlike anything Alfred had ever built. It looked like a race car, with no wheels.

"Wow!" exclaimed Reggie. "What is it?"

"That, my boy, is a Temporal Displacement Device." Uncle Alfred winked. "A time machine."

"Does it work?" Reggie asked, his mind racing with the possibilities.

Uncle Alfred shrugged. "Don't know. Never had the nerve to try it. Maybe I'm afraid it *will* work."

Reggie peered into the cockpit, his eyes bright with astonishment. "Can we try it?" he asked.

11

Happy that his nephew was still interested in his inventions, Uncle Alfred smiled. "I'm afraid not," he said. "But I will show you how it's *supposed* to work." And with that, he spent the next half hour going over the controls, showing his young nephew the ins and outs of time travel à la Uncle Alfred.

"Now, you've got to promise me that you won't tell anyone about this," the old man said when he'd finished. "And you mustn't fool with it when I'm not around. No telling what could happen."

Reggie promised, but in the days ahead his thoughts kept returning to the amazing time machine. What if it really *did* work? Wouldn't Uncle Alfred want to know? The more he thought about it, the more enticing the prospect became. He didn't like the idea of breaking his promise, but he knew that if the machine worked, his uncle would be too happy to be angry.

And so, that weekend, when his uncle was away, Reggie pried open the rusty old lock on his uncle's garage. Rushing inside, he threw off the tarp, opened the hatch of the time machine, and climbed inside.

12

"Well," Reggie said, his heart pounding, "here goes nothing." Taking a deep breath, he reached forward and flipped the ON switch in the center of the instrument panel.

Alfred was furious when he realized someone had broken into the garage. But his fury turned to horror when he saw his temporal displacement device, with smoke wafting out of the charred cockpit. "Reggie!" he gasped, staring at the remains of his now-useless time machine. "I never should have trusted such a curious boy!"

With a determined step, Alfred marched across the street to Reggie's house and knocked on the front door. Reggie's father answered, a pleasant smile on his face. "Hello, Alfred, what can I do for you?"

"Tell your son, Reggie, to stay out of my lab!" Alfred blurted.

"Alfred, what are you talking about? I don't know anyone named Reggie, and you know as well as I do that Clarice and I don't have any children."

Alfred stared in horror at the man who would have been Reggie's father, realizing that his time machine had actually worked. But the worst part was that Alfred knew he'd never be able to get Reggie back. For the only copy of the machine's plans were with Reggie, hidden under the cockpit seat!

Baby Fat

erald Bolton stared up at Brenda, his gaze making her vaguely nervous. "You're a chubby one, aren't you?" she asked, leaning over the ten-month-old baby boy's crib. Ever since the Boltons moved in next door, Gerald had become the newest and most frequent client on Brenda's baby-sitting list. Now, as she watched Gerald, Brenda remembered the first day she'd met his mom and how strange she'd thought the woman's baby-sitting instructions were.

"Under no circumstances are you to touch the child," Mrs. Bolton had instructed her. "If he cries, just turn on the tape deck and he'll quiet down." She'd then demonstrated by playing not a soothing lullaby but a series of wild electronic screeches.

Brenda had winced at the horrible racket.

To each his own, Brenda had thought. "But what if he needs changing?" she'd asked Mrs. Bolton. "I have to touch Gerald then, don't I?"

"He won't need changing," Mrs. Bolton had said flatly, a thin smile creasing her face.

And she'd been right. Not only did Gerald never need changing, but he'd stop crying every single time he heard that awful tape.

Brenda had heard the same weird music coming from the Bolton home at all hours of the night. She had

14

also noticed that Mrs. Bolton took Gerald somewhere every day at the same time—5:30 P.M.—without fail.

"Is there something wrong with you?" Brenda asked the odd little boy she was hired to watch until Mrs. Bolton returned to take him to the doctor. "Probably nothing a soft touch couldn't fix, huh?" She looked at her watch. "Well, it's getting close to 5:30. Your mommy will be here soon. *She* touches you, I hope."

The baby did nothing but stare at Brenda, making her feel guilty for not reaching out to him. Surely it couldn't hurt to touch him just once. She'd read that babies needed human contact.

She was just starting to reach out to the child when she heard Mrs. Bolton come in the front door.

"We're off to see Dr. Mallory," she said, scooping up the baby. Then she looked at her watch. "And we're going to be late. Just gather up your things and let yourself out, okay, dear? I've got to rush."

Curious, Brenda watched as Mrs. Bolton drove off with Gerald. Then she made up her mind. She was going to find out what was going on.

Quickly rummaging around until she found the doctor's name and address in Mrs. Bolton's address book, Brenda tore out of the house, leaped on her bicycle, and arrived, huffing and puffing, at the doctor's office not too long after Mrs. Bolton. After hiding her bike behind some bushes, Brenda crept up to one of the office windows and peeked in.

There they were!

Careful to duck out of sight whenever necessary, Brenda watched as Mrs. Bolton and Dr. Mallory hovered over Gerald.

15

"I don't know what to do anymore, Doctor," Mrs. Bolton said, a worried look on her face. "Gerald eats everything I give him and he still begs for more. I've got five traps set already and it's not enough!"

The doctor placed a sympathetic hand on her shoulder. "It is quite normal at this stage. Give him whatever he wants. As for the food supply, I can help you there. I just got in a new shipment."

The doctor went over to a small cabinet, opened it, and pulled out a cage of mice. He removed one, held it over Gerald's open mouth, and dropped it in.

Brenda stumbled away from the window. *The baby ate the mouse!* Her mind reeled in horror. *Whole!*

Grabbing her bike, she raced home and ran up to her room. It was crazy. It just *couldn't* be true. What she'd seen was some kind of waking nightmare. But what if it wasn't? What if the Boltons were some kind of mutant family, some kind of alien race bent on taking over the world? She thought of the weird music Mrs. Bolton had played for her and her fears mounted. She had to report this to the authorities, but first she needed proof. She would wait until her next time to baby-sit and get a picture of Gerald . . . at mealtime.

The next day, with her parents' camera hidden in her backpack, Brenda waited until Mrs. Bolton left the house. Then she grabbed her camera and searched for the cage of mice. Finding it under the kitchen sink, she swallowed her nausea, pulled one of the squirming creatures out, and brought it into Gerald's room. "Here you go, you little creep," Brenda said, holding the rodent over Gerald's gaping mouth.

In a flash, the baby's tongue flew out and wrapped not around the mouse, but around Brenda's wrist! It yanked her down with surprising strength.

"LET ME GO!" she yelled, trying to pull herself loose. "I'll get you more mice, I promise."

But the baby ignored her pleas and began sucking on her fingers. Brenda was in a wild panic as her hand disappeared into the baby's ever-widening mouth. Soon she was in up to her elbow, her body flooding with pain as the child's powerful digestive juices began dissolving her skin.

An hour later, Mrs. Bolton walked into Gerald's room in time to see Brenda's feet disappearing into the baby's mouth. She reached for the phone. "Hello, Doctor? Yes, everything's fine. I just had to tell you that Gerald's just started on grown-up food!"

The Book of the Dead

he rain slashed down out of the slate-gray sky so heavily that it sounded like a million marbles bouncing off the roof. Sarah Quiller stared out the window through the torrent of water at a world that appeared to melt and ooze down the glass. She sighed. She had nothing to do.

Turning from the rain-streaked window, Sarah went to find her mom watching television in the family room. "Can I go to the library?" she asked.

"Honey, it's pouring out," her mom replied. Why don't you watch TV with me?"

Sarah scowled, then tried another tactic. "I have to return a book or they'll charge me a late fee."

"Oh, all right, but bundle up. I don't want you getting sick."

"Thanks, Mom," Sarah said, throwing on her raincoat and running out the door.

The rain felt cool and delicious against her face as she dashed the five blocks to the town's ancient library. It loomed ahead, looking like a scary gargoyle hunched on the small hill overlooking the town. Long ago, the building had been the home of the wealthy Crowley family, which had an enormous book collection. When the last Crowley died, the home was donated lock, stock, and books to the town, which promptly turned it into a library.

Sarah loved the moldy old place. She could spend hours poring over hundreds of volumes, hardly aware of the passage of time. Now reaching the library's wide porch, Sarah pushed open the heavy door, with its ornate brass knocker, and disappeared inside.

There at the front desk sat old Mrs. Ballinderry, her beady eyes squinting at Sarah, who dashed for the stairs. On the second floor was the Crowleys' ballroom—Sarah's favorite part of the old place. That's where some of the oldest and most interesting books were kept.

Sarah frowned, spotting the same old titles staring back at her. Why did it always take so long for the library to get anything new?

Frustrated, she walked out into the hall where she saw a door marked NO ADMITTANCE. That was odd. She'd spent half her life in this place and never noticed it. Curious, she walked over to the door and turned the knob. It was locked.

Shaking her head, she turned and found herself nose to nose with the ancient librarian.

"What are you doing here?" Mrs. Ballinderry screeched, her voice tinged as much with fear as anger.

Sarah stifled a scream as she looked into the old lady's bulging eyes, their whites yellowed and bloodshot.

"I—I was—"

"No one's allowed in there without permission! You'll have to leave." Mrs. Ballinderry paused for a moment, as if gathering her rage. "In fact, I think it's best if I didn't see you at this library for at least a month!"

Sarah tried to argue with the old woman, but it was no use, and she finally bowed her head and left.

19

"How dare that old bat ban me from the library," she mumbled angrily as she walked home in the pouring rain. "And for what? Being curious? Isn't that what the library is for?"

And then it hit Sarah. Obviously, something *extremely* important was behind that locked door, and Sarah was determined to find out exactly what it was. As she continued to walk home, she devised a plan. She would go there tonight after the place was closed. She'd noticed that one of the basement windows was broken, and that's how she'd get into the building. Once inside, she'd figure out a way to get into that room and see what all the fuss was about.

The rain just kept coming down, and it was still pouring that night as Sarah crept past her mother, who was dozing in front of the TV. Ever since the divorce, her mom worked the late shift in a diner, and to unwind, she'd usually watch a bit of a late movie before going to bed. Often she'd never make it to her bedroom. Usually Sarah felt bad, seeing her mom exhausted and conked out like that, but tonight she was glad. Except for one heart-stopping moment when Sarah's foot had hit a loose floorboard her mom had hardly stirred, so getting out of the house had been a cinch.

Once she'd carefully eased the door shut behind her and was outside and in the clear, Sarah broke into a run. As she headed down the block toward the library, her feet slapping against the layer of slick, wet leaves covering the sidewalk, her heart pounded with excitement.

As she grew closer to the library and saw its forbidding towers, she began to wonder if this was such a

20

good idea. Then she recalled Mrs. Ballinderry's pruny face and her anger renewed. She'd get in that room, just to spite the old witch.

It took only a minute to find the unlocked window, and even less time to find the old skeleton key, carelessly stored inside Mrs. Ballinderry's unlocked desk drawer. Snapping on her flashlight, Sarah raced up the steps to the second floor, pass key in hand, and inserted it into the lock. The tumblers turned with a satisfying click, and the door creaked open.

Sarah's eyes widened as she swept the beam of her flashlight around the dusty room. Except for one lone table and chair, the room lay completely empty.

Then she saw the book. Large, ancient, and leather-bound, it sat on the table as if on an altar of worship.

Approaching the table, Sarah suddenly felt scared. *Get out of here!* her inner voice screamed. But Sarah ignored the warning. She'd come too far to quit now.

Sitting down in the chair, she opened the book and frowned as she saw what lay inside.

Names, nothing but names—hundreds of them.

Looking closer, she saw that the book was some kind of record of the town's deaths. It began in 1701, when the town was founded, and continued right up until the present day. The funny thing was, the handwriting looked *exactly* the same all the way through.

Sarah stared at the very last entry: *Terrence Hardwyn, October 23, 1995, Heart Attack.*

Thinking back to only a week ago, Sarah recalled when Mr. Hardwyn, the school principal, had collapsed in his office. He'd been a nice man, and she'd been saddened to learn of his death.

21

Sarah was just about to close the book when she noticed a change in the space below Mr. Hardwyn's name. At first it appeared to be an ink stain spreading across the page. But, no, somebody, or some*thing*, was actually writing . . . right before her eyes!

Gasping, Sarah backed away from the book as the invisible hand wrote another name in that same, spidery script: *Sarah Quiller, October 30, 1995, Accident.*

Sarah ran from the room, her screams echoing through the old building as she tore down the stairs

and blasted through the front door. Oblivious to the torrential rain and everything around her, she darted out into the street. The police officer, responding to the library's silent alarm that Sarah had set off when she'd entered the building, didn't even have a chance at stopping his patrol car in time. He slammed on the brakes, putting the cruiser into a spin. Hurtling out of control, the car skidded on the wet leaves, knocking Sarah into the air. Her lifeless body hit the pavement with a muffled thud.

Horrified, the young policeman, Officer Robert Toland, jumped out of his cruiser and stood staring at Sarah's broken body, his tears mixing with the rain. He gazed into her eyes, eyes forever frozen in a look of unbridled terror, and knew that his career was over.

Devastated with grief and guilt, Toland stumbled back into his cruiser and radioed for an ambulance. He replayed the moment over and over in his mind. Why hadn't he turned into the library's driveway as he'd planned? Why couldn't he have swerved into the building instead of hitting her? Why? Why? WHY?

Endless questions ran through Toland's tortured mind as he waited for the ambulance to arrive, questions he knew would haunt him for the rest of his life. The town's clock struck midnight, thunder rumbled, and his tears flowed anew as he reached for the revolver at his side. He never heard the cackling laughter that echoed through the library, nor did he see that invisible hand write another name right below Sarah's: *Officer Robert Toland, October 31, 1995, Suicide.*

Behind Door Number Two

Margie couldn't believe her eyes. "Hey, Bobby, come look at this!" she shouted.

Margie's little brother tromped up the stairs. He found his older sister in the back of her huge walk-in closet. "What?" he asked. "You find a dead mouse or something?" Bobby, having just turned ten, was fascinated by anything dead.

Margie scowled at him. "No, butterball, I found a secret room."

Now it was Bobby's turn to scowl. "Yeah, right," he said, as he scanned the closet. He looked into his sister's sparkling eyes with a wary expression on his face.

"Give up?" Margie asked, smiling smugly.

When Bobby nodded, she reached up and pushed what appeared to be a knot in the wood. Something clicked and a panel slid open.

Bobby's eyes bulged. "Whoa, radical!"

But her brother's initial wonder turned to disappointment when he got a look inside the tiny, airless room. Dark and featureless, it held nothing but a few balls of dust and a cockroach that skittered across the floor.

"Aw, it's nothin' but an empty room," he moaned.

"What did you expect? Blackbeard's treasure?" Margie asked.

"Maybe a skeleton or two," Bobby replied, smiling impishly.

Margie shook her head, laughing in spite of herself. "Why not something practical, like that new baseball mitt you had your eye on down at Felson's Sporting Goods?"

Bobby's eyes lit up. "Yeah, I wish I had one of those!"

The panel to the secret closet whooshed shut, and through the cracks surrounding the opening, a strange red light spilled out, pulsing gently. Then, just as quickly as it had appeared, the light vanished and the panel slid open again.

"What's going on?" Bobby whispered, his mouth gaping.

Margie stepped forward, her heart racing. She peeked into the tiny room and gasped. "Bobby! Look!"

Squealing with delight, Bobby scampered into the room and picked up the brand-new pitcher's glove, its leather gleaming in the dim light.

Margie just stared—first at the glove, then at her brother—in shock. How had that happened? And better yet—could it happen again?

"Come out of there, Bobby," Margie said with urgency in her voice. "I wanna try something."

Bobby scooted out of the room, and Margie found herself even more nervous than before. "I wish I had one of those deluxe phone/answering machines," she said, her voice an excited whisper.

Once again, the panel whooshed shut and the red light pulsed. Margie could hardly contain herself while she waited for the panel to open. When it did, she saw exactly what she'd asked for—a brand-new phone with a built-in answering machine.

"All right!" she shouted.

"Nuts!" Bobby said. "This glove's got a rip."

"Oh, stop whining," Margie scolded. "My phone's got a chip in the plastic. Who cares? We got the stuff for nothing!"

In the next few days Margie and Bobby indulged their wildest dreams, and the secret closet delivered every item they asked for. Bobby got an expensive

mountain bike and a baseball autographed by Mickey Mantle. Margie got a pretty gold necklace and all the clothes she craved but could never afford. Like the glove and the phone, everything had some kind of imperfection, as if all the goods came from some cosmic reject pile.

But Margie and Bobby were having too much fun to care. Besides, everything was free. Unfortunately, though, their fun came to an abrupt end a few days later. Their parents had called them into the living room to talk about where they'd gotten all their new stuff.

"Where did you kids get the money for all of these things?" their mother asked, her eyes creased with worry. "This stuff is expensive."

"Your mother's right," their father added. "The two of you couldn't possibly afford all this with the allowance we give you."

Margie stole a glance at Bobby. He looked scared, but nodded to her that it was okay to tell. After all, it was the truth.

"Bobby and I found a secret closet in my room," Margie said, taking a deep breath. "Whatever we wish for just appears in there."

Their father shook his head. "I'm disappointed in both of you. After all we've done for you, you repay us with a lie even a five-year-old wouldn't believe." He looked sternly from Bobby to Margie. "You're both grounded for one month, and I want the truth about all this loot right now."

"But I told you the truth!" Margie cried.

Angry and frustrated, she stormed up to her room, kicking the door shut behind her. It wasn't fair! She'd told them the truth and they'd treated her like some kind of juvenile delinquent.

"I wish that stupid closet would go away!" she screamed.

Just then, Billy walked into the room. "Hey, what's that ticking sound?" he asked. "You ask the closet for a clock or something?"

"What are you talking about?" Margie asked. "I didn't ask for . . ." But her voice trailed off as her eyes grew wide with the sudden realization that she *had* just wished for something.

"Oh, no," she cried, dashing to the closet and seeing the pulsing red light. She quickly punched the knot in the wood with her finger, then stifled a scream as the panel slid open . . . revealing a huge bomb sitting in the center of the secret room. The loud ticking echoed through the room as the timer wound its way toward zero, just seconds away.

"I take my wish back!" Margie shouted.

But no one heard her, as the enormous explosion turned most of the neighborhood into a smoking crater.

The Perfect Mom

Mrs. Levin flashed her high-wattage smile and offered Stephen and Brian more cookies.

"Thanks, Mrs. Levin," Stephen said, scooping up another delicious cookie. He stuffed it into his mouth. *Cinnamon heaven,* he thought as the tangy flavor exploded on his tongue. *Boy, Brian sure has the perfect mom.*

Grabbing another cookie, Stephen watched his friend's mother putter around the kitchen, humming softly to herself, her movements a homespun ballet. *That's how a mom ought to be,* he thought sadly. *Mrs. Levin is nothing like my own mother.*

For the last year his parents had been arguing and screaming at each other, over what Stephen didn't know. Every time he tried to find out the problem, his parents would give him these strange looks and tell him everything was okay. Finally, he'd simply started to spend as much time as he could at the Levin home. Here he found peace, quiet, and contentment.

"These cookies sure are great, Mrs. Levin," Stephen said, smacking his lips. "Great!" he repeated, though he didn't quite know why, since he'd already made his point.

"Why, thank you, Stephen, you're so nice to say that."

Stephen blushed and turned to his best friend, Brian, who was staring at his mother, as if studying her.

He caught Stephen looking at him and said, "You wanna go out and shoot some hoops?"

Stephen nodded. "Sure," he said. "I'm game."

Mrs. Levin turned from the sink, smiling. "Have fun, boys—fun boys."

A look of alarm flashed across Brian's face as he snatched his basketball from under the table. A moment later his troubled expression was gone, replaced by an eager smile.

"Everything okay?" Stephen asked, looking at his friend's face.

"Sure. What could be wrong?" Brian asked nonchalantly. He snapped the ball to Stephen and the two boys dashed out into the twilight.

Brian played like a boy possessed, his eyes glittering and the sweat trickling off his thick, brown locks as he made shot after spectacular shot. "Come on, Steve-o," he said, dribbling the ball through his legs. "I'm going to have to find some *real* competition."

Stephen smirked, snatched the ball, then made a perfect shot from the foul line. Retrieving the ball, he tossed it to Brian. "Your mom is great, you know? I wish my mother was like that."

Brian ignored Stephen and took another shot. Stephen found it strange that Brian never liked to talk about his mother. If he had a perfect mom like that, he'd talk about her all the time. He was about to tell Brian just that when Mrs. Levin walked over with another tray of milk and cookies. As always, she was smiling.

"Would you boys like more cookies—more cookies—more cookies—more cookies—more cookies?"

Brian turned to Stephen, panic in his eyes. "Go home," Brian ordered. "My mom is sick."

Stephen just stood there, dumbfounded, as Brian tried to pull his mother into the house. But she just stood there, with that perfect smile on her face.

"Dad!" Brian shouted.

The screen door banged open and both Brian and his father guided Mrs. Levin back inside the house.

Stephen frowned. What the heck was going on here? With curiosity overriding everything, Stephen crept up to the window and spotted Brian and his dad disappearing down into the cellar, guiding Mrs. Levin in front of them. Racing around to the back of the house, Stephen knelt down and peered through a basement window where some of the black paint on the inside of the glass had chipped away.

Stephen gasped and clapped a hand over his mouth as a scream rose in his throat. There, on a makeshift operating table, lay Mrs. Levin, her chest opened to reveal a galaxy of printed circuits and blinking lights. *Brian's mom is a robot!* Stephen's mind screamed. *No wonder she's so perfect!*

Sobbing with horror, Stephen raced home. How could he have been so stupid? How could he have missed the signs? It was all so obvious now. No *real* person could have been so perfect.

He found his parents in the family room. He sat on the couch, trembling. His mother was the first to notice his agitated state. "What's wrong, honey?" she asked, putting down her crossword puzzle.

His father looked up from some business reports, his eyes questioning.

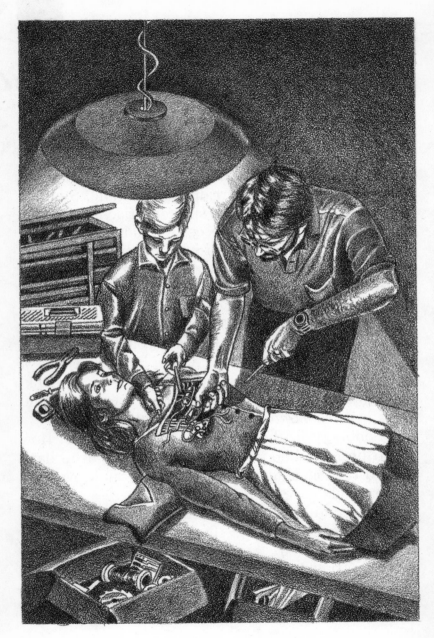

"I—I don't know how to say this," Stephen stammered, and then he just blurted it all out. "Mrs. Levin is a robot! She's filled with all kinds of wires!"

His parents turned toward each other, a worried glance passing between them. "We know, dear," his mother finally replied.

Stephen reeled back. "You know!" he gasped.

Stephen's father sighed. "Son, Mr. Levin works for the company that makes the robots. He was very supportive when . . ." He paused. "Anyway, with the new technology, there's hardly any difference in . . . that is, no one can really tell that—"

Stephen's mother glared at his father. "Now what are we going to do? If there are problems in Mrs. Levin there are probably going to be problems in—"

"Marybeth, please!" Stephen's father snapped. "Maybe the boy doesn't need to know!"

Stephen shook his head, confused. "Problems? What are you talking about?"

His mother reached out to him. "Oh, honey, we were going to tell you when you were old enough to understand."

"Understand what?" Stephen asked, frightened.

"We couldn't bear it when you were killed on that bicycle last year. So, we—"

"NO!" Stephen screamed. "You're lying! I'm as real as you are! I'm not a—" But the trauma of finding out what he was had short-circuited Stephen's brain, and all he could do was repeat, "Robot, robot, robot . . ."

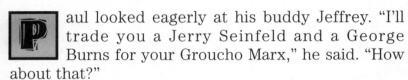

Meeting Mr. Evil

Paul looked eagerly at his buddy Jeffrey. "I'll trade you a Jerry Seinfeld and a George Burns for your Groucho Marx," he said. "How about that?"

"Those guys are still alive," Jeffrey said. "Groucho's worth a lot more than those two put together."

"All right, wait a minute," Paul said, turning the plastic pages of his loose-leaf binder autograph book. He just had to figure out a way to get that Groucho autograph. It would be a cool addition to his collection.

Watching Paul continue to flip through the pages, Jeffrey smiled as he thought of an irresistible deal. "I'll tell you what," he said, casually waving the Groucho autograph in the air.

"What?" Paul asked, his eyes fixed on the autograph.

"You get me Mr. Evil's signature and I'll make it an even trade." Jeffrey saw Paul deflate.

"Aw, man, nobody gets *his* autograph. He's like the Holy Grail."

And it was true. Mr. Evil, the nationally famous and reclusive TV horror-movie-show host and magician extraordinaire, *never* gave out autographs. Getting his signature would be worth a thousand Grouchos.

Still, Paul was determined to do it. "All right, Jeffrey. I don't know how, but I'm gonna get that autograph." A sly grin took over his face. "And you can keep your Groucho!"

That night, as he lay in bed, Paul thought about it more and more. Having Mr. Evil's autograph would be the crowning piece of his collection. He was so excited by the idea that by the time he fell asleep he'd already formulated a plan.

The next day after school, Paul put his plan into motion. First he took the bus to the TV station where Mr. Evil worked. Sneaking past the guard, he then went around to the back of the studio area and waited for nearly two hours before a technician stepped outside for a cigarette break. Then, as the man went to stub out the butt, he noticed the five-dollar bill Paul had planted. The scheme worked perfectly. As the technician walked over to pick up the money, Paul easily slipped inside.

When his eyes grew used to the dark, Paul crept forward, careful not to trip over the light stands and thick coils of cabling that lined the hallway.

"Hey, you!" a voice shouted.

Paul turned and saw a harried-looking man with a headset clamped to his head. "Yes?" Paul replied timidly, a shiver shooting down his spine.

"If you're looking for the *Bimbo the Clown Show,* it's across the lot in Studio B."

"Uhh, actually, I'm supposed to pick something up from Mr. Evil," he said. "Where I can find him?"

The young man in the headset sneered. "Oh, him. You'll find Mr. High-and-Mighty in his dressing room down the hall to the right. Better watch yourself, though," the young man said as he walked away. "He gets pretty hot-tempered sometimes."

Thrilled, Paul scurried off before the man got curious and returned. He found the dressing room door marked with a sad-looking cardboard star. Paul's heart raced as he put his ear to the door and heard someone mumbling to himself, the voice raspy and harsh. Wiping his sweaty palms on his jeans, Paul gathered his courage and rapped on the door.

The mumbling stopped. "If that's you, Harker, tell the union people to jump in the proverbial lake!"

"Excuse me, Mr. Evil, could I speak with you?" Paul said timidly.

"Go away!"

"Please, sir, I came a long way."

A split second later the door flew open and Paul's jaw dropped. Standing before him, dressed in tails and a black cape, was a tall, slim man with his face wrapped in a towel. Only his eyes showed, and they burned with an intensity that made Paul nervous. "I— I'm sorry, I was looking for Mr. Evil," Paul stammered.

The man frowned and continued to stare. Resisting the urge to bolt, Paul held out his autograph book and a pen. Curiously, the man's eyes softened. "Ah, one from my legion of fans," he said in a commanding English accent. "Well, do come in, my boy."

Paul followed the man into the dressing room, his eyes alighting on years of accumulated knick-knacks and show-business memorabilia. Mr. Evil sat at his vanity table and held out his hand. "The book, my child."

Paul handed over his autograph book and watched as Mr. Evil scrawled his name in large, flowing letters. Once finished, the man gave the book back and stared at Paul, his eyes looking him up and down. "How would you like to be on my show?"

"Really?" Paul said, his voice cracking with excitement.

"I need someone to saw in half during the break in the afternoon movie. The boy those union idiots sent over had no camera presence. But you have a look that will do quite nicely. Are you interested?"

"Definitely!" Paul exclaimed without hesitation.

The eyes behind the towel smiled. "Excellent. You will find a costume behind the changing screen. It should fit you. We go on in ten minutes. Oh, and one more thing. Do not come out from behind the screen until I tell you. Is that clear?"

It took Paul only a minute to throw on the costume and he began to grow impatient waiting for Mr. Evil to tell him he could come out. What was he waiting for, anyway? Was the old guy afraid Paul would see him without his makeup?

Tired of waiting, he came out from behind the screen and gasped. There sat Mr. Evil, the towel in his lap—and no face! There were muscles, tendons, and bone, but no skin. On the table before him, pinned to a Styrofoam head like the mask that it was, sat the leering, jowly face familiar to every kid in America: Mr. Evil. It looked strange sitting there, the bushy, pointed eyebrows frowning above the empty eye holes.

Instead of reacting angrily, Mr. Evil averted the horror of his ravaged face and said, "I'm sorry you saw that. It was a terrible accident many years ago. Do you still wish to work with me? I won't blame you if you don't."

Paul felt awful. He'd embarrassed the man. Walking bravely forward, he laid his hand on Mr. Evil's shoulder. "It would be an honor to work with you, sir," Paul said.

Mr. Evil nodded, a tear in his eye. Then he reached forward, grabbed the mask, and fixed it to his ruined face, smoothing it in place. In seconds Mr. Evil sat before him in all his glory, and Paul felt a tiny shiver of excitement run up his spine.

A knock sounded on the door and the man with the headset peeked in the room. "Places, everyone."

Paul followed Mr. Evil into the brightly lit studio. There on a raised platform was the box for the Sawed Man illusion. It had a large hole at one end for a head and two smaller holes at the other end for feet. There was also a slit down the middle to accommodate the saw. Paul climbed inside and Mr. Evil folded it closed, then latched it tightly. He leaned down and whispered to Paul. "Don't worry, my boy,

I've only lost one assistant." He laughed, and Paul smiled at the bad joke.

A moment later, the stage manager gave the signal, the red light on the cameras glowed, and Mr. Evil went into his act. Paul felt a thrill. *Wait till Jeffrey sees the show tonight*, he thought. *This is way better than a lousy autograph!*

Mr. Evil finished his introduction, then picked up the saw. "Are you ready, my young friend?"

Paul nodded and the saw began to make its way down through the box. Just as Mr. Evil had told him to do, Paul began moaning in mock pain . . . until he felt the cold steel slice into his belly.

"Stop, Mr. Evil!" Paul shrieked. "You're killing me!"

But Mr. Evil only grinned and sawed faster. "You're killing me, too, my child!" he said to the studio audience. And then he leaned in close and whispered to Paul, his voice tinged with sadness. "I'm sorry, dear boy, but I can't have you revealing my secret to the world, now, can I?"

Laughing in perfect Mr. Evil style, he sawed away as Paul shrieked and the small audience of children cheered.

In the control room, the director shook his head and turned to the producer. "Where does the union get off sending us these amateurs. That kid couldn't scream to save his life!"

I Dream of Genie

Marc found the old bottle sitting on top of a battered trash bin behind Thompson's Emporium. He was always finding cool stuff back there, and today's find ranked with the best of them.

Black as night, the faceted bottle had strange-looking writing etched into its crackled surface, highlighted with gold-leaf paint. Stuffed into its mouth was an ornate cork, complete with a red ribbon and a lump of sealing wax.

"What a neat old bottle!" Marc said, turning it over in his hands. "I wonder why Old Man Thompson threw it away."

He grasped the fat cork and tugged. With a quiet hiss the cork slid out, followed by a fragrance that reminded Marc of burning incense. Then, suddenly, the bottle vibrated in his hands and dark purple smoke shot out. In a heartbeat, there stood a tall, olive-skinned man dressed like an Arabian prince. He smiled, revealing pointed teeth, and then he bowed low.

"Master," he said, "you have freed Amir of the Golden Jinn. I am your servant for three wishes."

Marc's eyes dazzled. "Whoa! Like for real?"

The genie bowed again. "Command me, oh wise one."

Marc's mind raced. What should he wish for? A million enticing thoughts sped through his mind, clashing and competing with one another. But which three should he pick? They *all* sounded great.

Better test him with something safe, Marc thought. "Okay, I want to go to Disneyland," he announced, his mind conjuring up all the great rides.

The genie bowed, waved his hand, and disappeared in a flash of light. Marc frowned. Why was he still standing in this dirty, smelly alley? Why wasn't he at the amusement park?

Great, he thought, *I had to get an idiot for a genie.* Picking up the bottle, he trudged home, wondering if it would make a good candleholder.

But the next morning, Marc's parents bounded into his room, smiling and laughing. "Guess what," they said, bursting with excitement. "We're taking you to Disneyland today!"

"YES!" Marc cried, leaping out of bed. "The genie works!"

Marc and his parents spent the whole day at the park, going on every ride twice and gorging on all the food that was bad for him. As they drove home that afternoon, Marc felt pleased with himself. All in all, it was a good day . . . a perfect day! And with a genie, things were going to get a whole lot better.

That night, after his parents had gone to bed, Marc uncorked the bottle and the genie reappeared.

"Was your first wish satisfactory, Master?"

"It was fantastic!" Marc exclaimed. "I wish *every* day could be just like this one!"

The genie bowed. "As you wish, Master."

The next morning Marc's parents bounded into the room. "Guess what! We're taking you to Disneyland today!"

"Oh, joy," Marc said, trying to look excited. "Disneyland . . . again."

And just as he feared, the day unfolded *exactly* as it had the previous day, right down to the chocolate-ice-cream stain on his shirt. The only difference was that Marc now knew what was coming.

That night, he pulled the cork out of the bottle, but the genie did not appear. "Where are you when I need you?" Marc asked, looking inside the bottle.

Frustrated, Marc recorked the bottle, put it on his dresser, and went to bed.

"Guess what! We're taking you to Disneyland today!"

Marc's eyes snapped open, bulging in horror as they focused on his parents' happy faces.

"NO!" he screamed. "I—I'm not feeling well. I couldn't possibly go there feeling the way I do, no sir, no way."

His mother felt his forehead. "Oh, you're fine, honey. A day at the amusement park will do you good. You *love* those rides."

And no matter how much he protested, his parents insisted on taking him to Disneyland.

That night, desperate to break the awful cycle he had wished on himself, Marc tried to summon the genie again. He almost cried with relief as the familiar purple smoke flooded the room.

"Where were you?" he asked, not even trying to mask his annoyance.

The genie bowed. "Conferring with the infinite, Master."

Marc rolled his eyes. "Well, you sure left me holding the bag."

"What do you desire for your third and *final* wish?" the genie asked, ignoring Marc's comment.

A look of excitement mixed with desperation filled the boy's eyes. "I never want to have another single day like today for as long as I live! I want you to make it all *stop*!"

The genie frowned. "Are you sure, Master? I am not supposed to give people chances to reconsider their wishes, but in this case I—"

"I'm positive," Marc said, cutting the genie off.

"Very well," the genie said, raising his hand.

Marc felt tingly all over as the room went dark and he lost consciousness.

When he awoke, he found himself in his bed, with the morning sun shining in through the blinds. Raising himself up on his arms, Marc scanned the room, looking for the familiar black bottle. It was gone—and so was his nightmare. Relief flooded his heart, as he raised his eyes to the ceiling and said, "Thank you."

Suddenly, his bedroom door flew open and his parents bounded into the room. "Guess what?" they said, bursting with excitement. "We're taking you to Dis—"

Right in midsentence they stopped, their happy expressions frozen onto their rigid faces.

Panicked, Marc shot out of bed and dashed to the window. He whimpered as his worst fears were confirmed: The cars, the people, even the birds were all frozen as though they were in a giant photograph.

"No!" Marc shouted, as he turned and grabbed first his mother and then his father, willing them to move. But both of his parents felt like lifeless pieces of stone.

Collapsing to the ground, Marc began to cry. In his desperation to stop the day from its endless repetition, he'd gotten something much worse—a moment that would remain fixed forever, a moment that would leave him as lonely as the grave.

The Haunted High-Rise

arla stamped her feet in frustration, her blue eyes blazing. "But, Dad, you promised!" she whined. "You said this would never happen again."

"I know, sweetheart, but something came up and I have to go to the office," Carla's dad said sheepishly. "Besides, you can see the game on TV."

Carla pouted. "It's not the same."

She tried to stay angry, but her heart melted as she looked into her father's warm, brown eyes. "Look, honey," he said. "I know it hurts right now, and I wish I could spend more time with you, too. But the truth is, when you become a lawyer, you'll understand how precious time is." He shrugged. "Besides, time heals all wounds, and before you know it you'll forget all about this ball game."

No way am I going to forget the ball game, Carla thought unhappily as her father drove off. *But one thing I'm definitely going to forget about, and that's being a lawyer. I want to have time for my kids!*

But as much as she felt angry with her father, Carla also felt bad for him. It wasn't his fault he had to work all the time. It wasn't like he didn't *want* to go to the game with her.

Suddenly, an idea popped into Carla's head. She'd surprise her dad with a nice lunch that she'd deliver

45

personally to his office! Dashing into the kitchen, Carla began pulling food out of the refrigerator, and within an hour she had a picnic basket packed with a lunch of leftover chicken, potato salad, and pickles.

Perfect, she thought, surveying the lunch she'd prepared. *Dad'll love this.*

A little after noon, Carla stepped off the bus and immediately started shivering from the cold October wind that sliced right through her coat. Walking briskly, she found her father's office building a few blocks away. She craned her neck as she stared upward.

Built in the 1920s, the Enright high-rise stood just twelve stories tall and could hardly be called a high-rise by today's standards. But back in the Roaring Twenties, when it was built, the building had dominated the city's skyline. Now other buildings, far newer than the Enright, completely dwarfed it.

Smiling in anticipation, Carla pushed through the revolving doors into the dark, marbled lobby. She crossed to the elevators, stepped inside, and pushed the button marked 12. The doors closed with a whoosh and Carla felt that sinking feeling in her stomach as the elevator car accelerated upward. As it passed each floor, a little bell chimed. 9-Ding . . . 10-Ding . . . 11-Ding . . . 12-Ding . . . 13-Ding! Wait a minute. *Thirteen?*

The elevator slowed and the doors slid open, revealing a hallway that looked like something out of an old movie. But how could this be? Except for the lobby, the building had been completely modernized years ago. And besides that, *there was no thirteenth floor.*

Carla pushed the button for the twelfth floor, but the doors remained open. From somewhere down the

46

hall she heard music. It sounded tinny like some scratchy old record. A moment later she recognized the tune: "Happy Days Are Here Again."

Panic building inside her, she stabbed the DOOR CLOSE button with her finger, but the doors remained open.

Then the music got louder.

"Well, I'm not staying in here," she said, her fear turning to defiance.

Grabbing the picnic basket, she strode out of the elevator and trotted toward the stairs, confused at first because the lighted exit signs were gone. She raced down the steps and threw open the door to the twelfth floor, where her father's office was. He'd probably have an explanation for this whole thing—except the floor she looked at *wasn't* the twelfth floor.

Carla gasped as she recognized the surroundings. How could she be back on the thirteenth floor, a floor that shouldn't even be there in the first place?

The music sounded even louder now as Carla swallowed her fear and decided to investigate. She crept down the hall, passing offices cluttered with out-dated furniture. Everything had a thick coating of dust, and cobwebs hung from the tarnished brass hat racks and old-fashioned floor lamps.

Now the music was so loud Carla's ears began to throb. It was coming from the corner office. Slowly, she crept forward, and when she was standing before it, she placed her hand on the office's door. It was ice cold.

All at once, the music ceased. Praying that this was all some kind of nightmare, she tried the knob. It turned easily and she stepped inside.

48

Like the other offices, it was furnished and decorated in a manner popular in the twenties. But it was what sat behind the massive desk that snatched Carla's breath away.

A man, or what was left of a man, sat in a wooden swivel chair. Staring sightlessly out of clouded eyes, sunken deep into their sockets, he had the moldy remains of a business suit on . . . and the shirt was drenched in old, dried blood. The gun that had killed him still lay in his hand. Beneath his rotted fingers sat a yellowed newspaper spattered with blood, dated October 29, 1929. The headline screamed: STOCK MARKET CRASHES!

Today is October 29th, too! Carla's mind reeled. Somehow she'd been caught in a weird anniversary time warp, triggered by the stock market crash over six decades ago. Frantically trying to figure out what to do, Carla jumped as the music blasted forth again.

And then the man behind the desk began to move, his mouth cracking into a smile that revealed the stubs of teeth blackened by decay!

Screaming, Carla tore out of the room, her eyes half-blinded by tears. She stumbled into the elevator and, without thinking, pushed the button for the twelfth floor. Miraculously, the doors closed, cutting off the horrifying music.

Carla nearly cried for joy when the doors opened and she recognized the familiar decor of her father's law firm. She was safe at last! Taking a moment to calm herself, she straightened the contents of the picnic basket and walked out of the elevator.

"It was all some stupid dream," she mumbled on her way to her father's office. "It just *had* to be."

"Well, hello, sweetheart," her father said, smiling when he saw her standing in the doorway. "This is a wonderful surprise!"

Carla resisted the urge to fly into his arms. "I brought you lunch," she said, trying not to burst into tears.

"That's just dandy. Why don't we eat at the desk and we'll catch some of the game on the radio. How about that?" he asked, flipping on the stereo.

"Great," Carla said, unpacking the chicken. But her calm shattered as the tinny strains of "Happy Days Are Here Again" blasted out of the speakers. Immediately, the room blurred as the illusion the man-thing had created returned to its true form . . . the corner office on the thirteenth floor. In horror, Carla realized that she had *never* left the room!

The man-thing who had masqueraded as her father turned from the window and began shuffling toward Carla, his movements creaky and spastic. "I—I ran out of time," he croaked, his eyes wild and hungry. "Give me yours!"

Terrified, she watched as the zombie-like man edged closer, his hands reaching out to grab something you can't grab onto, something that was very precious and that she had no more of—time.

The Idiot Box

arry slammed down the phone. "Hey, everybody!" he yelled to his family excitedly. "We just won a new TV!"

"That's wonderful, dear," his mother said. She turned to Barry's father. "Isn't that terrific, honey?"

Sitting at the dining room table, Barry's father, intent on the model airplane he was building, nodded.

Arlene looked up from her schoolwork and gave her brother a withering glance. "Oh, come on, Barry, people don't just call up and give away TV sets. You have to enter contests and stuff."

"No, you don't. The guy said that we'd been picked to try out a new kind of television and that the demo unit was free for a one-month trial period."

"They didn't ask us to sign up for anything, did they, sport?" his father asked, suddenly concerned.

Barry shook his head. "No obligations."

His father shrugged and returned his attention to the model. "Well, I suppose it couldn't hurt to have another idiot box around."

The next day a black van pulled up to their house, and two men wearing black coveralls approached, pushing a dolly that held the biggest box Barry had ever seen. Friendly and efficient, the two men had the new TV unpacked and set up in minutes. One of them, a tall man with white hair and an accent Barry couldn't place, handed him the remote control.

"Be sure to turn on the set at precisely eight o'clock," the man instructed. He paused for a moment. "That's when the special circuits will be charged up."

"Is it like 3-D or something?" Barry asked, his eyes wide with excitement.

The white-haired man glanced at his partner and then smiled at Barry. "It's better!"

"What about now? Can I watch it before eight?"

"Can it, Barry," Arlene said, cutting him off. "You heard the man. We have to wait until eight."

The white-haired man smiled at Arlene, nodded to his partner, and walked out the door. Seconds later, the black van pulled away from the curb and disappeared in a cloud of exhaust.

Barry approached the new TV and ran his hands along its sleek black exterior. It looked and felt just like any other set, yet when he touched it he felt something strange course through his body, like a mild electric shock. Whatever was different about this TV, though, Barry had a feeling he was going to like it.

That night, the whole family gathered in front of the new TV, and at the stroke of eight Barry pressed the power button on the remote. The whole family gasped as the picture snapped on. Bright, saturated colors assaulted their eyes, and the sound was nothing short of astounding.

"I told you guys it was gonna be 3-D!" Barry shouted.

"It's absolutely breathtaking!" his mother said in astonishment.

Arlene stared at the TV and then at her family, wondering if they'd all lost their minds. The colors were

nice, but 3-D? No way! The picture looked just like any other TV. And what was so special about what they saw? It looked like some bad psychedelic light show left over from the sixties. The soundtrack was awful, too. Mindless, repetitive, and monotonous, it droned on and on, threatening to put Arlene to sleep. And yet her family sat enthralled by it all. What on earth was going on?

Well, who cares if they like it? she thought. *I don't have to sit here and watch this junk, do I?*

Sighing in disgust, Arlene got up, went into her bedroom, and started doing her homework. Sometime later, she heard Barry calling her.

"Arlene, please come here, we wish to converse with you," he said, his voice flat and mechanical.

Arlene frowned. "'We wish to *converse* with you'?" she mumbled under her breath. "What is Barry trying to pull?"

More than a little curious, she left her room and walked into a nightmare. Her parents and brother stood waiting for her with odd, hostile expressions on their slack-jawed faces. They started trudging toward her, their jerky movements like those of puppets.

"What are you doing?" Arlene said, starting to panic. "Is this some kind of joke?"

The new TV blasted, and suddenly Arlene saw something flashing so fast on the screen it was nearly invisible: KILL THE ENEMY! KILL THE ENEMY!

Arlene cringed in the corner as her family advanced toward her. "What are you doing?" she cried. "I'm not the enemy! I swear I'm not!"

But her parents and brother said nothing as they moved closer, their eyes completely glazed over.

"The TV!" Arlene gasped. Realizing that her only hope was to turn off the horrible thing, she dove across the carpeted floor and grabbed the plug.

But before she could yank it out of the socket, she felt her family's hands grasping her. Her helpless screams fell on deaf ears as her loving mother, father, and brother tore her apart.

* * *

The white-haired man smiled as he stared at the dozens of television monitors on the wall. Except for some minor glitches, everything had gone exactly as planned with all twenty-five test families. He swiveled in his chair and faced the audience of military men and government officials before him. One of the army generals, a stout man with cold eyes, spoke up.

"What about others like the girl?" he said, his voice tight with arrogance. "She was not affected."

The white-haired man smiled thinly. "There will always be a few, but like the girl, my dear general, they will be eliminated."

The general grunted and the others began to murmur among themselves. The white-haired man stood up, commanding everyone's attention.

"Gentlemen, please! Put your worries behind you. Once the Orwell Television Device is perfected and installed in every home, the populace will be in our complete control. We will have an army of puppets who will follow our every command. And all our new army will have to do is keep watching the idiot box! Welcome, gentlemen, to the Brave New World!"

And with that, the whole room roared with laughter.

The Mummy's Ring

As the bus hissed to a stop in front of the museum, Mrs. Hutchins eyed the students. "I expect everyone to be perfect ladies and gentlemen and to stay together at all times. Is that clear?"

Everyone droned back, "Yes, Mrs. Hutchins."

Roddy shook his head and whispered to his best friend, Liam, "Why did we have to get that old bat? This field trip's gonna stink, for sure."

Liam nodded absently as he stared out at the museum, his pulse quickening with excitement. He could hardly wait to see the new Egyptian exhibit, especially the mummy of Khafra, the last Pharaoh. Hailed as a major archeological find, Khafra's body had traveled from museum to museum all over the world. Ever since his uncle had given him a book about ancient Egypt, it was all Liam ever talked or thought about.

"Liam Reynolds!" Mrs. Hutchins shouted. "Did you hear me? It's time to go—*now!*"

"Sorry," Liam said, racing down the aisle and out the bus's open door.

Inside the museum, all the kids laughed and joked as they glided through the familiar exhibits. Roddy pulled Liam aside and nudged him in the ribs. "Hey, buddy, get a load of Claudia Aziza. Is she gorgeous, or what? I mean, she looks so exotic!"

Liam gazed at the prettiest girl in school. Just then she turned and fixed her luscious, chocolate-colored eyes on him and smiled. Instantly, Liam's legs turned to butter.

Roddy nudged him again. "Man, she's got it for you, big time!"

Liam felt the color rise in his cheeks. "Cut it out, Roddy. She's just being nice. Why would she want me?"

Roddy shrugged. "Who cares, kiddo? Like my dad always says, 'You've got to seize the moment.' "

And how Liam wanted to do just that. In his mind's eye, he was assertive, strong—in a word, irresistible. But the truth was, Liam had been too shy to approach any girl, let alone Claudia.

He was just trying to work up the courage to go over to talk to her when the class wound its way into the Egyptian room, and he suddenly remembered why he was excited to be there. There, in a glass case on a raised platform, lay the remains of Khafra, his regal face unwrapped for exhibition.

The class formed a circle around the mummy as the guide, an elderly Englishman, told the story of how the young pharaoh had lived, loved, and died.

"As a special part of our exhibit we have Khafra's ring," the guide added, pointing to a special case next to the mummy. "He and his bride, Khepri, exchanged matching bands on their wedding night. The rings were supposed to grant them immortality. Obviously, it does not seem to have worked."

The class giggled, and Roddy whispered, "What a dweeb!"

But Liam wasn't listening to Roddy or to the guide. He was watching Claudia as she glided toward the ring case, her eyes bright with fascination. *Could this vision of beauty really find me attractive?* Liam wondered. Ignoring the butterflies jittering in his stomach, he sauntered over to her, a look of cool detachment on his face.

"Beautiful, isn't it?" she breathed.

"Not as beautiful as you," Liam blurted out.

His heart hammered against his ribs as Claudia turned those devastating eyes toward him. "I—I'm sorry, that just came out," he said.

She smiled, revealing perfect teeth. "I am Egyptian. It is nice you are interested in the history of my people."

Relieved to be talking about his favorite subject, Liam said, "Yeah! Especially the story of Tutankhamen. Did you know—"

He stopped as Claudia leaned toward him and whispered, "You are the one."

"I—I am?" Liam stammered.

She smiled again, her eyes blazing. "Seize the moment," she murmured, then turned and left.

Liam knew exactly what she was talking about. He stared at the ring, his mind a raging torrent. *She wants me to steal it for her!* he thought wildly.

A few moments later, the class moved on, but Liam stood rooted to the spot, unaware of anything but the ring. Composed of a scarab design with intricate details carved into it, the ring had two blazing rubies that were its eyes. It was gorgeous—a ring fit for a pharaoh's queen—not to mention for the prettiest girl in the school. Liam *had* to have it.

Feeling giddy, he stretched his hand towards the ring case, then stopped. *What if I set off some kind of alarm?* he wondered. Then he looked back into the case and blinked. The ring had disappeared!

Panicked, he felt something on his finger. And when he looked at his hand, he had to stifle a scream. He was wearing the ring! Growing frantic with terror, he tried to pull it off . . . but it was stuck.

For the rest of the day Liam kept the hand with the ring on it in his pocket, and when he got home that night, he tried everything to remove it: soap, oil, Vaseline—everything! But the more he twisted and turned it, the more tightly the ring clung to his finger. And what was worse, the skin around the ring had turned a sickening greenish gray.

The next morning Liam's whole arm was gray . . . and it was growing paralyzed.

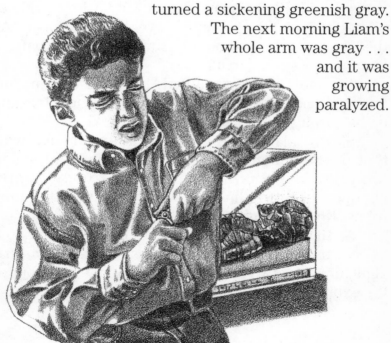

Terrified, he threw on his clothes, put his arm in a sling, and snuck out of the house. He took the bus to the museum and staggered into the building. Both arms were now useless, and his legs felt as stiff as wood. Liam hobbled into the Egyptian room. There, next to the mummy's case, stood Claudia. She smiled, her brown eyes glowing in the dim light.

"What have you done to me?" he cried.

"I haven't done anything," Claudia said innocently. "Like the guide said, the ring granted us immortality. I returned last year when my mummy was found and someone put on my ring. Now it is Khafra's turn to return to the living."

Liam approached the case where the mummy lay and saw that Khafra's face was now a healthy shade of pink. Suddenly, the mummy's eyes snapped open. As the life slowly drained out of Liam's body into Khafra's, the mummy sprang to life.

"Noooo!" Liam screamed. He tried to run, but found his body paralyzed, the ancient magic burning up his insides.

Slowly, Liam's live body began exchanging with that of the mummy's dead one, and suddenly Liam found himself *inside* the case, his body tightly wrapped in rotted linen. He looked out at the now-robust Khafra, holding Claudia's hand.

As the light faded from Liam's eyes, and the dust of centuries settled into his bones, he caught a final glimmer of the two lovers, walking hand in hand out of the exhibit room—vibrant, young . . . and immortal.

The Othermother

thermother here!" little Jimmy cried as Melanie walked into the room.

She sighed, annoyed. "What are *you* doin' up?"

"Othermother here!" Jimmy insisted. "Othermother! Othermother!"

Melanie strode over to the crib, her anger rising. "Look, Mom and Dad left me in charge here, and they're gonna get mad at *both* of us when they get home if you don't stop this nonsense and go to sleep."

Her little brother was eighteen months old and just beginning to talk . . . and talk . . . and *talk*. This "Othermother" business was his latest in a long line of gibberish. Melanie felt a twinge of guilt as she looked at the little guy. He stood, wide-awake and wide-eyed, clutching the wooden bars of his crib. *At least for once I can make out the words he's saying*, she thought. *Even though I don't understand what they mean.*

"Did you have a bad dream?" she asked, trying to sound sympathetic.

"No!" Jimmy cried. "Othermother *here!*"

Melanie sighed again. "Othermother, yourself. It's time to go to sleep, little brother." And with that she tucked the squirming toddler back under the covers.

But Jimmy sprang back up and pointed toward the old rocker sitting in the corner, the one their parents had found in the attic all covered with dust and cobwebs. The moonlight reflected off its fresh white paint, making it glow in the shadowy room.

"Othermother!" Jimmy said, staring at the chair as it rocked gently back and forth, as if someone had recently vacated it. Melanie stared at the chair too. Feeling a chill run up her spine, she turned back to her little brother and found the way he was staring at her unnerving.

"Enough of this, Jimmy," she said sternly. "Have you been out of this crib?"

The little boy shook his head vigorously, and Melanie felt stupid. Of course he hadn't. Jimmy could babble a mile a minute and drive everyone crazy, but no way could he climb out of his crib.

"Othermother," he whined. "Othermother! Othermother!"

"Go to sleep," Melanie said firmly. Shaking her head, she walked out of the room and closed the door behind her.

Back in her bedroom, Melanie turned on her radio and tried to tackle her homework. She usually did well in everything, but this year was different—*way* different. Ever since her family had moved into the old O'Malley house, all of her friends treated her like she was some kind of weirdo—as if it was her choice to move into this creepy old place. In fact, she hated it from the moment she stepped inside. But that wasn't the worst part. Her new friend at school, Maddy Blanch, told her what had happened in it years ago.

"It was in all the papers and stuff," Maddy had said. "Mrs. O'Malley's little boy died of some kind of weird disease, and she wouldn't let them take her son's body away. For days she just sat there next to his bed in her rocking chair, rocking back and forth and singing some creepy lullaby."

Melanie remembered how her pulse had quickened as she listened to Maddy. "What happened?" she'd asked her friend.

"The police finally came and took the body," Maddy had answered. "The next night, Mrs. O'Malley poisoned her husband's dinner. Then she went into the kid's room, sat in the rocking chair, and slit her own throat. They didn't find the bodies for a whole week!"

Her homework forgotten, Melanie now found her heart pounding as she sat at her desk remembering Maddy's story. Suddenly, she heard a strange melody floating through the air. It sounded far away and oddly beautiful. Cocking her ear, Melanie could make out a faint, whispery quality to the melody, as if another person were quietly whistling along in perfect harmony.

Springing up from her desk, she threw open her door, ran across the hall, and burst into Jimmy's room.

"Othermother!" he cried with glee, pointing to the rocker.

The rocker in the corner moved erratically, as if someone had just leaped out of it.

Melanie turned to Jimmy, her eyes blazing. "You're a bad little boy!" she cried. "You're playing tricks on me, aren't you?"

Jimmy's expression turned from a happy smile to a sulky pout. He shook his head and pointed to the rocker again. "Othermother," he said, smiling innocently. "Othermother!"

"STOP IT!" Melanie screamed. "I've had it with you!"

Frightened by his sister's reprimand, Jimmy began to cry.

"Fine. You go ahead and cry. Maybe you'll get tired and go to sleep." Shaking her head, Melanie stalked out of the room and slammed the door shut behind her.

Instantly, the crying stopped.

"Huh?" she said, turning back to the child's room. As she reached for the knob, the mournful singing she'd heard earlier began again, only louder this time. Her hands trembling, she twisted the doorknob, pushed open the door . . . and froze.

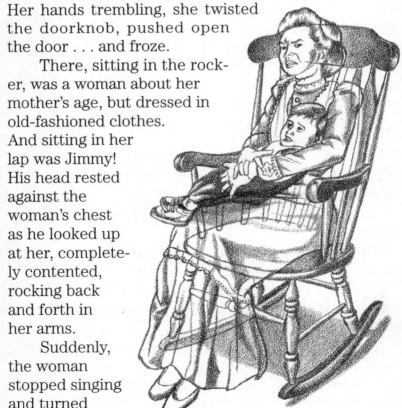

There, sitting in the rocker, was a woman about her mother's age, but dressed in old-fashioned clothes. And sitting in her lap was Jimmy! His head rested against the woman's chest as he looked up at her, completely contented, rocking back and forth in her arms.

Suddenly, the woman stopped singing and turned

64

toward Melanie, fixing her with a hostile gaze. Her eyes glowed red, like the embers of a half-dead fire, and her skin, even in the pale moonlight, looked mottled by some kind of grayish-green mold. The worst part was the horrible gash in her throat, its jagged edges spread wide, like some obscene grin.

"MINE!" the Othermother said, clutching Jimmy closer, her angry voice whistling through the gaping wound.

Melanie screamed and ran from the room. She flew down the wide mahogany staircase and out the heavy oak front door, nearly tripping on the front steps. Her heart pounding, she tore blindly down the street, tears of terror streaming down her face. She didn't know where she was going, and she didn't care. She only knew that she was never, *ever* going back into that house again.

She would never forget those blazing red eyes and that hollow, whistling voice as it echoed through the darkened house. Nor would she ever forget the happy smile on her little brother's face as he and the Othermother vanished into thin air, leaving the empty white rocking chair swaying ever so gently in the moonlight.

Revenge for Sale

I hate you, Evan! I hate you!" Patrick screamed, pummeling his older brother with his fists as they rolled around on the floor.

But then Evan grabbed Patrick's arms, flipped him over, and pinned him. "I told you to stay out of my stuff, you little squirt!" Evan snarled. "Say uncle, or I'll drop a gooey looey on your face."

"NO!" Patrick yelled, turning purple with rage.

Evan grinned, exposing a chipped tooth. "All right, you asked for it, little brother."

Patrick began to squirm as Evan let a particularly disgusting string of drool descend from his mouth, sucking it back up after coming within a hairsbreadth of Patrick's nose.

"Say uncle," Evan said, sneering, "or I'll let it drop all the way."

"No! Get off me, or I'll—"

"BOYS!"

As if jolted by an electric shock, the two brothers leaped to their feet, looking contrite as they met the fiery gaze of their mother.

"How many times do I have to tell you boys not to fight?" she said, her hands poised on her hips.

Patrick's eyes narrowed as he looked at his older brother. "He started it!"

Evan shoved him, knocking Patrick into a nearby table. A vase fell over, scattering flowers and dank-smelling water all over the floor.

"That's it!" their mother said, stabbing a finger into the air at them. "You two will go to your rooms right now! And no TV for a week!"

Patrick scowled as he trudged up the stairs and tromped into his room. He ignored the model plane he was working on and plopped onto his bed, sighing in disgust. Why did Evan have to be such a jerk all the time?

Pushing thoughts of Evan from his mind, Patrick picked up the comic book he'd been reading and began to flip through it. He laughed as he reached the small ads in the back for "X-ray" glasses and "genuine submarines."

A kid has to be a real dope to buy this junk, he thought.

Turning the page, Patrick frowned as his eye caught sight of an unfamiliar ad:

REVENGE FOR SALE

Life got you down? Bullies making you miserable?
Then Professor Maxon's Miraculous RETALIATOR Kit
is your salvation. Don't get mad—get even!
Satisfaction guaranteed, or your money back!
Only $19.95 plus postage and handling.
Please allow four weeks for delivery.

Patrick felt a small chill race down his spine as he reread the ad. Could it really be true, or was it some kind of stupid joke? Then again, people got into trouble for false advertising, didn't they? Excited, he scurried over to his bureau, snatched up his coin bank, and dumped its contents onto his bed. He quickly counted all the quarters, dimes, nickels, and pennies, dividing them into neat little piles. There it was, a grand total of $26.84. Not a fortune, but certainly enough for a RETALIATOR Kit.

Patrick smiled, his eyes filling with wicked delight. In a month or so, he'd fix Evan—but good!

* * *

The package arrived four weeks to the day later. Patrick sneaked it up to his room and tore off the plain brown paper wrapping. Inside, he found a jumble of electronic parts, a box to mount them in, and a thick booklet of instructions.

"Read all instructions carefully," it warned.

But Patrick ignored the warning and flipped to where the step-by-step instructions began.

Hours later, after the last connection was snapped into place and the batteries were inserted, the RETALIATOR was finished. Patrick studied his handiwork, frowning in disappointment. It sure didn't look like much. Smooth, black, and nearly featureless, all it had was a tiny red button and a lens-like opening at one end.

"I bet it's no better than those stupid X-ray glasses," Patrick muttered. Standing, he pointed the device at the F-16 model still lying uncompleted on his desk.

"To defy Zantar of Andromeda means death by disintegration!" he bellowed. "Take that!" Jabbing his finger on the button, Patrick recoiled as a bright scarlet beam of light lanced out of the box, turning his new jet plane model into a pile of smoking ash.

"Yikes!" he shouted, throwing the RETALIATOR onto the bed. He raced over to his wastebasket, fished out the crumpled instruction booklet, and began reading it. Apparently, the RETALIATOR, coupled with the mind of its user, could do just about anything. He'd have to be careful what he thought about. He wanted to make Evan suffer—not *kill* him. Excited, he ignored the page marked "Further Warnings," grabbed the RETALIATOR, and stalked into Evan's room. He found his brother hunched over his desk, tinkering with something.

"Hey, jerkface!" Patrick called. "Let's see how *you* like being the 'little' brother!"

Evan turned, saw the RETALIATOR aimed at him, and smiled. "I wouldn't do that, if I were you!"

69

But Patrick pushed the button anyway. It only took a second for Patrick to realize that something was terribly wrong. Screaming in horror, he watched as *his* body, *not* his brother's, began to shrink. Soon his voice sounded like nothing more than the high-pitched buzzing of an angry mosquito as he disappeared inside his clothes.

Evan stared at the empty mound of clothing and smirked. "Maybe next time you'll read the warnings, squirt," he said. Then, turning back to his *own* RETALIATOR Kit, Evan picked up the instruction booklet and began reading it out loud. "*Never* use the RETALIATOR on a family member, or the power will reverse."

Evan tossed the booklet away and picked up his own RETALIATOR, giving it a respectful glance. "Whoowee!" he said, smiling broadly. "These dudes don't mess around." Laughing, he reached for a screwdriver and resumed his tinkering, a smile of smug satisfaction on his face. If everyone else proved to be as stupid as Patrick, his dreams of world conquest would soon become reality. "Today, my little brother; tomorrow the world!"

Me and My Shadow

I have a secret I must tell, a secret that will chill your hearts and lie coiled in your brains like a poisonous snake ready to strike. For, like me, *you* are all in terrible danger.

It began on a day when the sun hid behind a mask of clouds and fog hung like a shroud over the land, a day I should have stayed indoors. I remember running from the house that afternoon, my mother's angry voice ringing in my ears. I had played hooky from school again and had no desire to listen to her reprimands—whether I deserved them or not.

Feeling as free as a bird, I ran across the yard, laughing at the world and all its stupid rules. I was heading for the vacant lot, where I hoped to find Stinky and the guys playing softball. But all I found was nothing. With nowhere else to go, I went to the pond where we swam in warmer weather. But there was no one there, either.

On the pond's muddy shore was a huge granite boulder that we called Black Rock. My science teacher told us that the rock was pushed down from Canada during the last Ice Age. It jutted out over the water, and I always found it peaceful sitting on top of it, pitching stones into the placid water.

"Where the heck is everybody?" I asked myself, climbing the huge rock and looking out over the pond.

"*Hey, Bram!*" someone called.

I turned my head, expecting to see one of the guys, but I saw nothing. I frowned, feeling decidedly creepy, since the voice sounded like . . . well, like it had come from directly behind me.

"Who said that?" I called out.

"*Braaaaaaaam!*" the voice called again, stretching out my name like a piece of taffy.

"Okay, guys!" I yelled. "Give it up!"

Silence.

"I'm gonna give whoever it is a knuckle sandwich if you don't cut this stuff out!" I threatened.

"*Down here, Bram,*" the voice said, almost a whisper now.

Glancing down, all I saw was my shadow. "Down where?" I asked. "Hey, this isn't funny."

"*Here, stupid,*" the voice hissed.

And then I saw my shadow wave . . . all on its own!

Shrieking with fright, I tumbled backwards off the boulder and scrambled to my feet. My shadow mirrored every move I made, then leaned against the boulder and crossed its arms. My arms hung limply at my sides, and I was getting really scared—especially when I realized that it wasn't sunny out and I shouldn't even *have* a shadow.

It spoke again. "*How would you like to be in two places at once, Bram?*" it asked. "*Would you like that?*"

"Huh?" I grunted, totally confused.

My shadow threw up its hands. "*Oh, don't be*

72

*such a doofus. How would you like to do whatever
you want while everyone thinks you're in school?"*

Suddenly, I understood. "You mean you'd—"

"Exactly," said the shadow. *"Now, come over
here and grab my hand."*

Puzzled as to how I could do that, I approached
the boulder and reached out. Amazingly, a solid hand
emerged from the moss-covered stone and grasped
my fingers. I grabbed ahold and pulled out of the rock
my exact twin—my shadow reborn as a human!

"Ah, this feels great," my shadow said, clapping
his arms around himself as though seeing if he was
real. Then he looked at me and smiled mischievously.
"Why don't I go home and take your punishment for
you? If I'm not mistaken, there's a matinee down at the
Bijou you've been dying to see."

I found myself returning my shadow's devilish
grin. "All right!" I shouted. "This is cool!"

My shadow's face then turned serious. "Just make
sure you're back before dinner so we can switch back.
Can't have you having *all* the fun, now, can we?"

In the days that followed, I got to do all the
things that kids wanting to play hooky have only
dreamed about. I went to the movies every day, spent
hours fishing, and played video games for hours. But
after a week, I'd done and seen everything. I was
actually getting bored with too much freedom!

"I want to go back to school," I told my shadow,
unable to believe what I heard myself saying.

"I don't know, Bram," my shadow said, frowning.
"I kind of like it out here in the real world. It has its
advantages. We have a girlfriend now."

73

This caught me by surprise. "We do? Who?"

"Only Pia Swenson," my shadow said proudly.

"Pia Swenson! She's never given me the time of day."

My shadow, his eyes cold and calculating, said, "I know."

"But how did you do it?"

"Come closer and I'll tell you."

It was a stupid thing to do, I now know. I walked over to my shadow, and his hand shot out and grabbed me by the arm. His touch felt ice cold and damp as the grave. I screamed in pain as I felt a bolt of fire shoot through my body. In an instant, I found myself staring out from behind a gray wall. My former shadow had transformed *me* into *his* shadow!

"I'm sorry, Bram, I really am," my shadow said, gloating at his triumph. "But I couldn't go back to being a mere shadow, not when the world of light has so much to offer. But don't think I'm unappreciative. We'll *always* be together."

And so we have been. I've followed my shadow everywhere. I've watched him graduate from school, go to college, and grow up to marry Pia Swenson. I've watched him live the life he stole from me, and now, finally, my chance is coming to take my life back.

You see, my shadow and Pia recently had a child— a son. Now I'm just waiting for the right moment to pull the same trick on the boy that was played on me . . . and return to the world of light once again!

Mistaken Identity

he three boys stood behind a hedge, their eyes wide with imagined horror as they watched Old Man Laszlo shuffle up the walk to his house.

"Aw, he's just a harmless old man," Ronny said, his expression turning skeptical.

"Yeah, Tommy Albert's disappearance doesn't have a thing to do with that old man," Jake sneered.

Alvin felt his face redden. "I'm tellin' you guys, Old Man Laszlo is a vampire! Take a look at that!"

The other two boys followed Alvin's gaze as an ambulance drove up and two attendants carried a complicated-looking piece of equipment to the house. They rang the bell and were admitted a moment later.

"These guys show up three times a week with that weird gizmo," Alvin whispered. "I peeked through the window one night and saw them hook Laszlo up to it. His blood went in one end of the thing, came out the other, then went back into his other arm."

"Whoa!" Jake gasped, his eyes as round as saucers.

Ronny sneered, still not convinced. "Yeah, so what?"

"I'll tell you, so what," Alvin snapped. "You ever notice that Laszlo only comes out after dark, and that the shades on his windows are pulled during the day? How about the fact that all the pets in the neighborhood keep disappearing? Well, he must've gotten tired of dog and cat blood 'cause I saw him throwing out some clothes that looked like Tommy's, and there was blood on 'em!"

"So, what're we supposed to do?" Ronny asked. "We can't exactly call the Bloodsucker Police."

Alvin didn't even crack a smile. "We're gonna wait until daylight and get him."

Jake blanched. "You mean—"

"Yep. A stake right through the old ticker."

"Get outta here," Jake said. "You're gonna sneak into Old Man Laszlo's house and drive a stake into his heart? You're nuts, Alvin."

"Do you want him to get *you* next, Jake?" Alvin asked. Then he turned to Ronny. "Or how about your little sister, Ronny? You're always saying she's a pain. Maybe you'd like Laszlo to take her off your hands?"

Jake shook his head and began to walk away. "If you wanna get rid of 'Count Dracula,' you'll have to do it yourself. I'm outta here."

Alvin turned to Ronny, who shrugged. "Sorry, Alvin," he said, running after Jake. "You're on your own."

"Chickens!" Alvin shouted after his friends. "I'll show you guys! I'll do it myself!"

And he *would* show them, Alvin told himself. His dad had a woodworking shop right in the garage—perfect for making a nice, sharp stake. He stared at Laszlo's house, imagining the creepy old man rattling around inside. "I'll get you, you old bloodsucker," Alvin muttered as he turned to walk away. "Just you wait."

The next day, Alvin pretended to be sick and waited for his parents to leave for work. Then he went into the garage and made a long, pointed piece of wood that would serve as his vampire-killing stake. With the sun high overhead, he left the garage, his stake in one hand and one of his father's old hammers in the other.

Bolting across the street to Laszlo's house, careful not to let anyone see him, Alvin found the old man's extra key under the front mat and snorted in contempt. *How could a vampire survive for hundreds of years and be so stupid?* he thought, then carefully slipped the key into the lock.

Once inside, Alvin found the house swathed in darkness. His stomach in knots, he crept up the stairs. Then, standing outside of Laszlo's bedroom, Alvin held his breath and pushed open the door. The old man lay huddled under the blankets, as silent as the grave.

That's odd, Alvin thought. *Why isn't the old goat in a coffin?*

Suddenly, Laszlo snorted and moved.

He's waking up! Alvin's mind screamed.

Darting to the bed, Alvin quickly pounded the stake into the old man's chest. Blood spurted everywhere as Laszlo shrieked in pain and clutched Alvin's arm.

"Why have you done this to me?" the old man cried. A moment later, he fell over dead.

Alvin stared at the body, drained of all its color. Afraid to stay another second, he wrenched himself free from the old man's grasp and ran out of the house. Back home, he stayed in his room, trembling with fright, until his parents called him for supper.

"Did you hear?" his mother asked the minute Alvin sat down at the table. "Someone killed poor old Mr. Laszlo. Can you imagine? He survived World War II, then kidney failure, only to be murdered in his bed."

Alvin's stomach twisted and the room spun. He'd been wrong! The machine he'd seen Laszlo hooked up to was for kidney failure! He pleaded illness and ran from the table, sure that he'd killed an innocent man.

In his room, Alvin lay sprawled on his bed. All he could see was the blood spurting and Laszlo's tortured face as he died. Exhausted from the day's ordeal, Alvin dropped off into a troubled sleep.

Around midnight, he awoke with a start and saw Laszlo step out of the shadows near his bureau. Dried blood stained the old man's shirt, and his eyes glowed red. Slowly, as if in a dream, he glided over to Alvin's bed.

"But I thought I—I killed you," Alvin stammered.

"I wanted you to think that. You and your little friends were becoming far too curious about my affairs. Now, regretfully, I must move on."

"B-But the kidney machine!" Alvin cried.

The old man smiled, revealing fangs poised to strike Alvin's throbbing jugular vein. "Meet a vampire with a kidney problem!" Laszlo threw his head back and laughed evilly. Then he quickly became serious as he fixated on Alvin's neck. "Alas, my boy, you didn't kill me. You see, to kill the undead you must pierce the heart." Laszlo smiled wickedly. "And you missed!"

The Initiation

he Marauders stood outside the marble mausoleum, their black leather jackets gleaming in the pale light of the full moon.

"You think he's gonna show, Kenny?" Homer Rodale asked, his reed-thin voice sounding impatient.

Kenny Forbes moved the half-chewed toothpick from one side of his full-lipped mouth to the other and squinted into the distance. "Yeah, he'll show. Everyone wants to be a Marauder."

Another few minutes went by and Mickey Peters nodded toward the wrought-iron front gate.

"Here he comes," he giggled. "Here comes old Bobby boy."

Bobby Landers, loaded down with a sleeping bag and what appeared to be a cooler, tentatively walked toward them, trying to avoid hitting the tombstones along the way.

"Oh, man, this kid is Dweeb City. Why'd you ask him to join, Kenny?"

Kenny smirked. " 'Cause he moved in next door to me and I thought we might have some fun with him. But don't worry, by the time we're through with our *special* initiation, he won't want to come within a mile of any of us."

The others chuckled as their innocent victim approached.

"Hi, guys," the boy said, a nervous smile on his face.

The Marauders stifled a laugh as Kenny stepped forward. "You sure you're ready to be a Marauder, Landers?"

The boy stood straighter, his chubby face taking on a defiant look. "I'm ready," he said.

Kenny nodded to Homer, who quickly picked the lock on the mausoleum, using tools from his locksmith father. The iron door swung open with a shrill squeak that set everyone's teeth on edge. Bobby Landers picked up his gear and, with a sigh of resignation, walked in. Homer slammed the door after him, snapping the lock back into place.

"Hey!" Bobby yelled. "You didn't say anything about being locked in! Wh-what if I have to go to the bathroom?"

All the boys standing outside the mausoleum burst into laughter as they started to walk away. "You'll have to hold it, Landers. You don't want to upset the zombies, do you?" Kenny called back. Then he whispered to the others, "We'll give him time to get settled, then really give him a scare. Mickey, did you get those masks?"

Mickey nodded and pulled out a particularly gruesome zombie mask, complete with rubber maggots poking out of the face.

"All *right!*" Kenny said. "This is gonna be fun."

Two hours later, the Marauders were back, now disguised as zombies. Homer began moaning and pounding on the door, and the others joined in. The effect was immediate. Bobby Landers began screaming for help as if his life depended on it. Kenny laughed and egged on the other Marauders to moan even louder. Everyone really poured it on, screeching and poking their faces through the door's wrought-iron bars, and holding the flashlights under their chins so that the beams would cast terrifying shadows onto the masks.

Suddenly, one long, horrifying scream came from inside the mausoleum, then . . . silence. Kenny held up his hand for quiet, and the Marauders cocked their ears, waiting. But they heard nothing, only the sighing wind and the hoot of a lone owl. Something wasn't right.

Frowning, Kenny nodded to Homer, who picked the lock and swung open the door.

"Oh, no," Kenny groaned as his flashlight beam fell on Bobby's body slumped against the wall, a look of terror frozen on his tear-stained face.

Rushing inside, everyone's worst fears were confirmed when Mickey touched Bobby's wrist and felt no pulse.

"No, no, no, no," Mickey kept repeating as he backed away from the body.

"Shut up!" Kenny hissed. "Shut up, all of you!"

Tired of taking orders from Kenny, Homer grabbed him and slammed him against the marble wall, his voice cracking from fear. "How could this happen, Kenny? How could a twelve-year-old kid drop dead like that?"

Kenny shook his head, not wanting to believe what had happened. "I—I don't know," he stammered. "Maybe he had a weak heart." Then anger flooded his body. "He should've known better than to come out here if his ticker was bad! He *knew* what to expect. It's not our fault!"

"What are we gonna do?" Mickey whined.

Kenny paced, thinking furiously. The answer came to him when he spied an empty hole in the crypt. Not even bothering to think why the hole was there, he blurted, "We'll put him in there." He pointed a shaking finger toward the crypt. "No one has to know."

Homer's eyebrows shot up. "Are you nuts? We've got to tell his folks. We can't just—"

Kenny stared at Homer, his eyes burning with fury. "Use your head, dummy! If we tell what happened, we're liable to be put in jail. Do you want that?"

The others shook their heads.

"All right, then," Kenny said solemnly. "Give me a hand with him."

Working quickly, the Marauders stowed the body in the empty crypt and ran out of the mausoleum as fast as they could.

Back at the old toolshed that served as the Marauders' clubhouse, the boys tried to calm down. But how could they forget about a murder? That's what it was, plain and simple. They'd scared Bobby Landers to death.

After an hour of nervous conversation and a ton of useless suggestions as to what to do, the boys finally decided they'd better just go home. But as they walked toward the door, someone began pounding on it, and everyone jumped a mile.

"W-who is it?" Mickey asked.

"Why don't you answer it and find out?" Kenny said, scowling. "It's probably just one of our parents looking for us."

"Wh-what if it's the cops?" Homer asked.

"If it were the cops, they'd bust the door down," Kenny said, rolling his eyes. "Now answer it, will you?"

No one moved.

"All right," Kenny said, marching toward the door. "*I'll* open it. You guys are a bunch of chickens."

Pushing Homer aside, Kenny reached for the wooden door and threw it open. Stifling a scream, he stumbled backwards, his eyes bulging from their sockets. There, in the doorway, stood Bobby Landers, and behind him stood three decaying zombies.

"I brought my new friends," Bobby said stiffly, looking through dead, glazed-over eyes. "They want to be initiated as members, too!"

Don't Open the Door

hunder rumbled through the house and rain slashed against the windows as Ralph's mother hung up the phone.

"Cindy's sick," she said to Ralph's father. "We'll never find another sitter now."

"We can always stay home," his father offered.

"It's my parents' fiftieth wedding anniversary. We *have* to be there."

"I can stay by myself, Mom," Ralph chimed in.

Ignoring Ralph's offer, his mother turned toward his father, his face buried behind the paper. "Honey, please put the paper down and listen to me."

Sighing, Ralph's dad tossed the paper to the floor, where it fell open. Ralph caught sight of a glaring headline:

"HATCHET MAN" KILLER ESCAPES FROM STATE ASYLUM!

Knowing that his parents would never let him stay home alone if they saw it, Ralph quickly picked up the paper, folded it, and placed it neatly on the coffee table. He looked at his father. "Come on, Dad, please?"

"Why should we trust you?" his mother asked. "You've never minded us in the past. At least with a sitter you won't open the door to just anybody. What about the time you let in that teenage hoodlum who ransacked the whole house? Or the time you bought a vacuum cleaner from that traveling salesman?"

Ralph smiled weakly. "I promise I won't open the door. Besides, no one will be out on a night like this."

Ralph's mother frowned. "That's not the point." She turned to her husband. "What are we going to do?"

"Sweetheart, how can we expect our son to grow up and take responsibility if we never let him?"

Ralph found his heart beating faster. Were they actually going to let him stay home by himself?

"All right," his mother said, fixing Ralph with a sober gaze. "You are to stay indoors and do your homework. Is that understood, young man?"

Ralph nodded, barely able to suppress his glee.

"After your homework, it's sack time."

"But, Mom—"

Her nerves already frazzled, Ralph's mother waved her hands in the air. "Fine, fine, stay up as long as you want. But don't open the door—to *anyone*."

Ralph gave his mother a puzzled look. "Who's going to come around at this time of night?" he asked, his mind flitting for a moment to the newspaper headline he'd just read.

"Never mind that," Ralph's father said. "With all the crazies out there, you can never tell. Just do as your mother says."

Later, Ralph watched as his parents gathered their coats and left the house. Then, just as the door clicked shut, Ralph leaped into the air and shouted, "I'm free! Free to do anything I want!"

Dashing through the house, he cranked up the stereo, snapped open a can of soda, and threw himself onto the leather couch. He was right in the middle of his favorite action show when suddenly someone began pounding on the front door.

Snapping off the TV, Ralph listened as the pounding grew louder, echoing through the house. He slowly crept toward the door and, standing with trembling limbs before it, peered through the tiny peephole. But the front light was burned out and he couldn't tell who it was.

"Wh-who's there?" he stammered.

"Got a delivery here for you," came the muffled answer.

Ralph frowned. "Leave it on the front steps."

"Have to get a signature," the voice insisted.

His heart pounding, Ralph couldn't decide what to do. His parents had been expecting a gift for his grandparents that hadn't arrived in time for the party. *Maybe that's it*, Ralph's mind raced. *Maybe the gift is finally here*. Tentatively, he reached for the deadbolt, but stopped when a tiny voice told him that it was far too late for a delivery. He crept over to a window, pulled back the drapes, and saw someone huddled under a raincoat.

Suddenly, lightning flashed and Ralph could have sworn he saw a shiny hatchet clutched in the figure's hand. Ralph gasped. Was it his imagination, or was the Hatchet Man standing on his front porch?

"Go away!" he screamed. "Or I'll call the police!"

Dashing to the kitchen phone he snatched up the receiver. The line was dead. *The Hatchet Man's cut the wires!* Ralph thought in a panic. *What am I going to do?*

The back door rattled and Ralph jumped as he saw a muddy hand streak across the glass. *How could he get there so fast?* Ralph wondered.

Screaming in blind panic, he decided he had to get to a neighbor's house to call the police. His heart pounding, he headed for the front door. With his hand nearly on the doorknob, he suddenly heard the back door open and wet footsteps squeaking across the kitchen's linoleum floor.

The killer's inside! Ralph's mind screamed. *But how did he get inside without breaking the glass?*

He was just about to turn the front doorknob when the doorbell rang. Wrenching open the door and starting to run out, Ralph stopped, dead in his tracks, his eyes wide with shock as he looked up into the face of ... his mother!

"We told you not to open the door, young man," she scolded. "How can we trust you if you don't do as we say?" She marched in, closing the door behind her.

His father strolled in from the kitchen. "That's right, son. We're very disappointed in you."

"Mom? Dad?" Ralph looked from one parent to the other in disbelief. "You—you mean it was you all along?"

But before his parents could answer, his shock turned to rage. "What do you mean, I shouldn't open the door?" he practically yelled. "I thought there was a murderer in here!"

"A murderer?" his mother exclaimed.

"Yeah, I mean when you cut the phone lines, I panicked, but the muddy hand really sent me over the edge!" Ralph cried. "What was I supposed to—"

"Muddy hand?" asked his father.

Ralph's mother looked puzzled. "Cut the phone lines?"

But before Ralph could respond, the doorbell rang.

Shaking her head in exasperation, Ralph's mother went to answer it. "Yes, who is it?" she asked impatiently.

"Delivery," came the muffled answer.

A chill ran down Ralph's spine. "Mom . . . uh . . ."

"Well, it's about time the present got here," his mother said, her hand on the doorknob. "Too bad it didn't arrive in time for the party."

"Mom, don't!" Ralph screamed.

But he was too late. His mother had already flung open the door and never saw the shiny hatchet as it hurtled toward her.

The New Kid

All eyes and gangly limbs, the new kid stood in the classroom doorway. Mrs. Browning smiled and beckoned her inside. She took a few halting steps into the room, then stopped, suddenly aware of the blatant stares of the other boys and girls.

"We won't bite," Mrs. Browning said warmly.

"Not before lunch!" someone shouted.

The class broke up with laughter. Even Mrs. Browning grinned as she rapped her desk for silence. "Okay, everyone. I want you all to give a hearty welcome to Linda Walters."

A few students groaned, others giggled, and still more rolled their eyes. "Hello, Linda!" the class said with machine-like precision.

The new kid said nothing, then slid into a seat, sitting face forward, straight-backed and unmoving.

"What is it with this kid?" Jessica whispered to Rob. "She acts like a real nerd."

Rob, a boy with kind blue eyes and a ready smile, shook his head. "How would you like to be her, not knowing anyone?"

Jessica shrugged. "I'd probably hate it, but at least I'd try and be friendly."

"Maybe she's shy," Rob offered. "I sure would be if I were the new kid."

During recess, he found her watching a game of dodgeball, a serious look on her pale face. "Hi," he said. "I'm Rob Devins. You're in my social studies class, with Mrs. Browning."

"I'm Linda," the girl said, her expression unchanged.

Rob smiled, but before he could respond, Linda asked, "What is this activity?"

"You're kidding. You've never heard of dodgeball?"

"No. What is its purpose?" she asked, her face a mask of studied calm. "It does not seem right to hit people with a ball."

Rob frowned, then offered a wry grin. "Lighten up, Linda. The purpose is to have fun."

"Fun," Linda said, mulling this over. "Thank you, Rob. I will try to remember that."

Rob felt sorry for Linda. He supposed that she must have moved from some isolated farm community where games like dodgeball were unknown.

"Would you like to go to a party with me tonight?" he asked, trying to be nice. "Veronica Malton is having a Halloween party. A lot of us are going."

Linda looked puzzled. "Halloween?"

Rob's eyes widened. "Now, don't tell me you don't know about the coolest holiday of the year. You get to dress up in costumes and be anything you want. Besides, Veronica's mom always has tons of food!"

Linda stared at the ground. "I do not know what to be," she said stiffly. "I have no costume."

Now you've blown it, you idiot, Ron thought. *Poor kid can't afford a costume*. "You know, you could just come as yourself," he said, smiling.

For the first time Linda smiled. "Good idea, Rob."

Rob beamed. "Great! I'll see you there."

The party was in full swing when Rob arrived in his dashing pirate costume. There were orange and black streamers, pumpkins galore, and a few cardboard skeletons taped to the walls. Rob spotted Veronica, dressed as a witch. She smiled and ran to him. "You look great," she said, flirting like crazy.

Rob scanned the crowd. "Have you seen Linda?"

Veronica scowled. "That new kid? I hope she's not coming. You didn't invite her, did you?"

Rob suddenly liked Veronica a lot less than he had a moment ago. "Yes, I did."

"Well, then, keep her away from me," she said, flitting away toward another group of kids.

"Love your witch costume," Rob called after her with a sneer. "It's so you!"

Shaking his head, Rob strolled toward the punch bowl. He picked up a glass, then put it down, suddenly angry. How could Veronica be such a creep? "If Linda doesn't show up," he grumbled under his breath, "I'm leaving this snotty party. On second thought, I'm leaving right now!"

Turning, Rob ran smack into someone wearing the ugliest, most realistic alien costume he'd ever seen. It had pale orange skin, two dark blue eyes, and a mouthful of long, sharp fangs. Rob gasped, then felt foolish. It was only a costume, after all.

"Gr-great costume," he stammered, walking away. "You really look out of this world."

"I am," a familiar voice answered.

Rob broke into a wide grin. "Linda! I thought you weren't going to wear a costume."

"You are correct," she said matter-of-factly. "I have come as myself."

Rob laughed. "You're funny, Linda. Now take off that mask so I can see you." He reached forward to take her hand. "Boy, these claws look so—"

But Rob's words caught in his throat when his hands met with warm alien flesh. Recoiling in horror, he screamed and stumbled into the refreshment table. Then the music, and all conversation, ground to a halt as a bright light from a hovering spacecraft suddenly streamed in through all the windows.

"You—you're a real alien!" Rob stammered.

Linda stepped forward, brandishing an ugly-looking weapon. "All subjects will remain calm until assimilation is complete." She turned to Rob, and he thought he saw a glimmer of sadness in those shadowy eyes. "I am sorry, Rob, but my planet is dying. The only way we can survive is to take your bodies for our own."

Rob cringed as other aliens like Linda began appearing. One horrid-looking creature approached Veronica, attached its claw-like hand to her head, and began melding with her body, like water into a sponge. She screamed in terror, her voice choking off abruptly.

Then suddenly Rob felt an alien claw latch onto him. "No, Linda, please," he whimpered.

Screaming, he felt the icy tendrils of the alien's mind lancing into his brain, embracing him with its cold, machine-like intelligence, destroying his mind . . . forever.

Index